W9-CBS-584

No, David!

By

David Shannon

SCHOLASTIC INC.

New York   Toronto   London   Auckland   Sydney
Mexico City   New Delhi   Hong Kong

To Martha, my mother, who kept me in line then,
and to Heidi, my wife, who keeps me in line now.

AUTHOR'S NOTE

A few years ago, my mother sent me a book
I made when I was a little boy. It was called
No, David, and it was illustrated with drawings of
David doing all sorts of things he wasn't supposed
to do. The text consisted entirely of the words "no"
and "David." (They were the only words I knew
how to spell.) I thought it would be fun to do a
remake celebrating those familiar variations of the
universal "no" that we all hear while growing up.

   Of course, "yes" is a wonderful word. . .but "yes"
doesn't keep crayon off the living room wall.

No part of this publication may be reproduced in whole or in part, or stored in a
retrieval system, or transmitted in any form or by any means, electronic, mechanical,
photocopying, recording, or otherwise, without written permission of the publisher.
For information regarding permission, please write to Permissions Department,
Scholastic Inc., 555 Broadway, New York, NY 10012.

This book was originally published in hardcover by the Blue Sky Press in 1998.

ISBN 0-590-93003-6

Copyright © 1998 by David Shannon. All rights reserved. Published by Scholastic Inc.
SCHOLASTIC and associated logos are trademarks and/or registered trademarks of
Scholastic Inc.

46 47 48 49 50   6 7/0

Printed in the United States of America   40

First Scholastic paperback printing, September 2000

David's mom always said...

No, David!

Go to

your room!

Not in the

house, David!

Davey,